W9-CAG-699

DUMB AND DUMBER

AN ORIGINAL STORY

IRRATIONAL TREASURE

By Steve Foxe

SCHOLASTIC INC.

CHAPTER 1

Let me tell you about the time Harry and Lloyd uncovered one of the biggest secrets in history, and how I ended up along for the ride.

Actually, I need to prepare you for Harry and Lloyd. You can't just start in with those two. If I try, you might slam the book shut. They're a *lot*, and this story is a LOT on top of that.

My name is Tini Hunter, and my best friend since preschool is Zoey Han. We're cool *now*, but we picked one of the worst times ever to have our worst *fight* ever. Not that there's ever a *good* time to have a giant fight with your BFF. But right before the deadline to choose buddies for the Washington, D.C., field trip? Historically (no pun intended) bad timing. It's only the *biggest* weekend in sixth grade, and we missed out on experiencing it together because of something so minor I can barely remember what caused the fight in the first place.

Before that blowout, our longest fight ever had lasted four days, two hours, and thirty-three minutes. I was counting on us patching things up with time to spare, but Zoey found another trip buddy and I ended up the odd girl out . . . which meant our teacher, Mrs. McCormick, made me the third wheel to a bicycle with more than a few screws loose.

So, instead of looking forward to a weekend of taking selfies in front of historic monuments with my best friend, I found myself cramped up in the back of the bus, trying my hardest to ignore the two most obnoxious boys in the sixth grade:

Harry Dunne and Lloyd Christmas.

I don't think I even knew their full names before Mrs. McCormick stuck us together. I just thought of them as . . . *those two*. The annoying ones. Dumb and Dumber—although I know it's not nice to call people names, even people who really get on your nerves. And besides, which one is Dumb and which one is Dumber? It changes by the second.

For your reference, Lloyd is the one with the bowl cut. Harry is the one who desperately needs a haircut. (Seriously, a bird could fly in there and *never escape*.) Got it?

Thankfully, I had an entire seat to myself, since we have an odd number of students in class. I think I might have dropped and rolled out of the emergency exit if I had to share a seat with Harry and Lloyd. Being in the same row was bad enough.

At first, I thought Mrs. McCormick put me in their group so she wouldn't have to pay as much attention to them. (Little did I know . . .) I am the responsible one, after all. That's why I always get picked to show the new kids around when someone transfers to our school. But Harry and Lloyd aren't new. They're just . . . well, how do I say this nicely?

I used to think Harry and Lloyd were typical class clowns, acting loud and strange to get attention. But about three hours into the bus ride to D.C. (which felt like three *days*), I came to understand that they're just this weird all the time. Like, naturally.

Let it be known that I *was* making an effort. I didn't really *want* to talk to them, but since we were going to be partnered up for the entire field trip, it seemed like the nice thing to do, right?

"So, have you ever been to Washington, D.C., before?" I asked them.

Lloyd's lips curled up in a grin, like he'd been waiting for this question since we boarded the bus.

"Legally, I'm not allowed to confirm or deny," he whispered, leaning across the aisle of the bus. "Let's just say . . . the Secret Service knows me by name. And I will *not* be allowed on the White House tour portion of the trip."

I had no idea if he was kidding or not. Either way, the grin didn't leave his face. I thought that there was a decent chance it was going to get stuck like that forever.

Lloyd leaned back into his seat, and I could see that Harry was really thinking about his answer.

"Hmm . . ." he said, staring off into space for what felt like an eternity. "I haven't been to Washington D, C, B, or A, as far as I know. But I'd have to ask my parents to be sure. How many are there, anyway?"

"How many what?" I asked.

"Washingtons," he replied.

For a second, I thought he was having fun at my expense—teasing the girl who got stuck with him and his buddy as a last resort. I laughed awkwardly, trying to play it off. But Harry just looked at me like he was really waiting for an answer. You know the way a dog looks at you when you're eating a big juicy hamburger, and it's hoping you'll drop some on the floor? Harry's got that expression *all the time*, only the dog in this case isn't too bright.

"Uhh . . . there's Washington, D.C., and Washington State; that's it," I responded, just in case Harry really didn't know.

"So there's only three—got it," Harry responded. He let out a big laugh and slapped his forehead. "No wonder it's hard to keep track. Whoever named them didn't even get their alphabet in order. They skipped *A* and *B*!"

"No offense, good buddy," Lloyd said, "but you sure are one pathetic loser. Who doesn't know how to count to *D*?"

So yeah, Lloyd and Harry really *are* this unusual. Talking to them has a funny way of running your brain in circles. I can't blame Mrs. McCormick for foisting them off on me.

(Oh, wait—I totally blamed her at the time. At least she gets *paid* to supervise them.)

Not that Harry and Lloyd were paying any attention for most of the bus ride, anyway. At one point, they got caught up in a contest to see who could hum at the same frequency as the bus motor. Their minds switched lanes faster than the bus driver cut through traffic.

"HUMMMMMMMMMMMMM" was all I could hear for about an hour of the trip, even when I stuffed my fingers in my ears. "HUMMMMMMMMMMMMMMM." The worst part is that neither of them was even close to matching the sound of the motor! It was just NOISE. I don't know how Harry did it, but he sounded just like that time my mom accidentally put Buddy's big rubber chew toy in the washing machine. Sixth graders shouldn't be able to make sounds like that.

If they keep this up all weekend, I thought, *I might see if I can get them shipped off to Washington, X.Y.Z., while I stay in D.C. by myself.* If only I knew the mayhem that awaited us . . .

Permission Slip

My Child _Lloyd Christmas_ has permission to join our class for a frield trip to _National Mall_.

With the following accomodations: _JUST TAKE HIM, PLEASE! I NEED A BREAK!!!_

Parent's signature _Mrs Christmas_

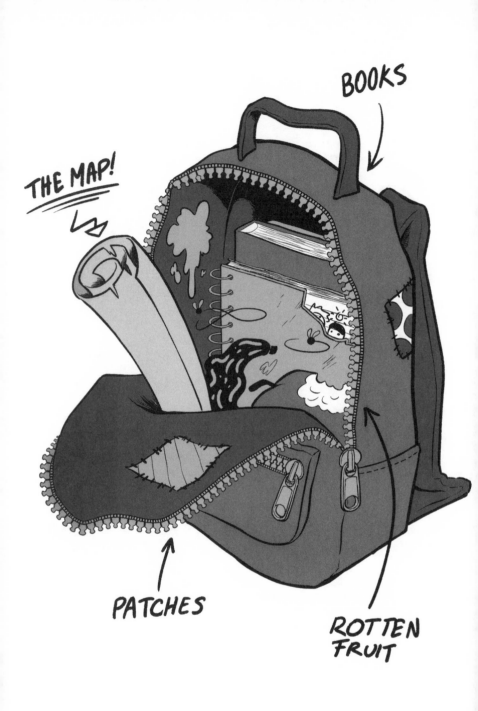

CHAPTER 2

My plan for surviving my long weekend with Harry and Lloyd was to keep my nose glued to the assigned trip journal, studiously taking notes about the natural world and our nation's long and eventful history.

That plan lasted about as far as the lobby of the Smithsonian National Museum of Natural History, the first stop on our trip. Upon entering one of the most celebrated museums in the country, what's the first thing Lloyd decided to do?

Crash some innocent Midwestern family's tour. And I don't mean he shadowed these unfortunate vacationers on their official tour—no, it was way worse than that. Lloyd directed this family of five around the museum's rotunda, giving them completely inaccurate information.

"As you can see, this woolly mammoth is from the rare southern hairless species," Lloyd said, pointing at what anyone who has grown up on planet Earth could plainly see is a regular taxidermy elephant.

AFRICAN BUSH
ELEPHANT

"Early man hunted them to make comfortable summer clothes, since northern mammoth fur was too hot to wear to the prehistoric beach," Lloyd continued.

He was standing directly in front of the plaque that says AFRICAN BUSH ELEPHANT in big letters, but somehow he had this family hanging on his every word.

"Not to mention itchy, eh?" he added, winking.

The entire family giggled, and for a moment, I wondered if Lloyd was going to wander off with them, taking on a new career as the world's least factual tour guide.

But just then, Mrs. McCormick put her hand on Lloyd's shoulder, dashing any dreams he might've had of mis-educating Midwesterners.

"Mr. Christmas, let's leave this nice family alone and stick to your assignment packet, why don't we?" she asked, only she wasn't really asking—she was commanding.

The confused family shuffled away, and I could tell one of them was going to look up "hairless woolly mammoth" later and feel very misled.

"Oh, right, right, right, the assignment packet," Lloyd said, patting his empty pockets. "I definitely didn't throw that in the garbage can on the way inside . . ."

Mrs. McCormick took a deep breath, and I counted my lucky stars that this trip didn't involve group grades. Luckily for Lloyd, though, Harry was looking out for him.

"I grabbed it, Lloyd!" Harry said, proudly pulling Lloyd's folded-up packet out of his backpack. Even standing ten feet away, I could spot several stains on the wrinkled set of papers, and I honestly couldn't tell you if those came from the trash can or from the depths of Harry's bag.

As Lloyd wrote his name on the corner of the soiled packet, Mrs. McCormick turned to me. I wasn't used to the expression she had on her face. Normally, teachers smile when they see me. *Oh, Tini, great job on the quiz!* they might say. Or *No surprise to see you've gone above and beyond yet again.* Or even once, *Really, Tini, you didn't have to do extra homework—you're making the other kids look bad.*

Only this time, Mrs. McCormick's face was set into a rock-hard glare.

"Tini . . ." she said, pausing between her words. "I'm trusting you . . . to keep an eye . . . on Harry and Lloyd."

Mrs. McCormick looked back over her shoulder, to where Harry was lifting Lloyd up to try to touch one of the elephant's tusks. I figured we had about ten seconds before security rush-tackled them, so I was mentally urging Mrs. McCormick to start speaking faster.

"I know it's not fair of me to ask, but—"

She didn't finish her sentence. Instead, she whipped around to tell the boys to knock it off. Only, by the time she reacted, Harry had already lost his balance. He and Lloyd landed on top of each other, their assignment packets fluttering away from them across the museum floor.

"Oh man," Harry said, his face pressed against the tile by one of Lloyd's shoes. "No wonder this mammoth outwitted all those prehistoric hunters. He's one slippery dinosaur!"

Mrs. McCormick didn't turn back to face me. She just stared off into the middle distance, her eyes unfocused.

"Two more years until retirement, Lin," she said as she walked away from us. "Just two more years, and you'll never have to think about them again . . ."

Maybe that was the attitude I needed to make it through the trip, I thought. *Two more days, Tini. Just two more days, and you'll never have to think about them again.*

Lloyd and Harry were busy untangling themselves after their failed tusk-outreach attempt, so I politely made my way past other museum visitors to collect their packets.

(I can't help it—even when it comes to these two knuckleheads, I'm a nice person. I also didn't want to get kicked out of one of the world's most respected museums for littering.)

Using two fingers, I picked up Lloyd's stained packet, which was now coated in a nice collection of dirt from its trip across the busy museum floor.

There was a man standing on Harry's packet, though. I'm surprised I didn't notice him sooner. Even with Lloyd and Harry causing a commotion, this stranger stuck out in the crowd. He was tall and broad and had one of the biggest, bushiest mustaches I'd ever seen. He was also wearing an expensive-looking trench coat with the collar popped up and pulled tight around his face, which might explain why he was sweating buckets. Seriously—it was kind of cold in the museum's entryway, but this guy looked like he'd just stepped out of a sauna.

"Excuse me, you're standing on my" — I almost said "friend's," but caught myself — "*classmate's* packet, mister."

The sweaty man stared down at me, his eyes half-blocked by his mustache.

"Forget you saw my face, child," he said, before turning around and rushing off into the crowd. This should have left more of an impact on me, but you have to understand—I was several hours deep into being paired with Harry and Lloyd. Nine out of ten doctors recommend limiting your daily exposure to these two.

I dusted off Harry's packet, which was still in better shape than Lloyd's despite the big footprint on its front cover.

"Who was that cool dude?" Lloyd asked. He appeared so silently and suddenly behind me that I couldn't help but jump.

"I liked his mustache," Harry added. "It reminds me of a squirrel."

Why was I even surprised that Harry and Lloyd thought the strange, sweaty, mustached man seemed cool?

Just two more days, Tini, I kept repeating in my head. *Just two more days.*

CHAPTER 3

Once the whole class was through the line and Lloyd had stopped wandering off to misinform tourists, Mrs. McCormick laid out the rules for this stop on the trip. Every group had two hours to explore the museum and complete the questions in our packet. We were supposed to stay with our trip buddies—no exceptions (unfortunately).

Zoey hadn't acknowledged my existence since our fight, but I was staring laser beams into the back of her head. If she felt her ponytail heating up, that's why. Instead of learning about precious gems and ancient cultures with her, I was stuck making sure Harry and Lloyd didn't attempt to free the taxidermized animals or something.

After two hours, we were all supposed to meet back at the African bush elephant (or hairless woolly mammoth, if you're Lloyd) to take attendance and visit the next museum.

I could see Zoey point at the sign for the live butterfly

garden, and I knew instantly that that was the *last* place I wanted Harry or Lloyd to notice. Those insects deserved better than these two invading their habitat. So instead I pushed them toward the ocean hall.

"Hey, fellas, want to see a really, *really* big whale?" I asked, breaking out the same voice I use when I do volunteer educational skits for the kindergartners. "Maybe you can stare at it for two hours while I fill out the worksheet questions on my own, huh?"

Lloyd let out a laugh and nudged Harry to laugh along with him, but I could tell Harry didn't know what was supposed to be funny yet.

"Oh, sweet, simple Tini," Lloyd said in a voice that made me want to feed him to the stuffed whale. "Museums are just like nightclubs or dentist offices—all the good stuff is behind the velvet ropes."

Lloyd pointed over his shoulder with his thumb, toward a sign that very clearly read NO ENTRY: STAFF ONLY.

"We have to sneak in there to see the exhibits Mr. Smith Stonian keeps to himself."

I took a second to consider correcting Lloyd on how the Smithsonian got its name, but I knew it wouldn't be worth the effort. Instead, I reminded him what words like "no" and "staff" mean.

"Lloyd, this isn't like when Harry mistook Mr. Friedfeld's janitor closet for the boys' bathroom," I said, recalling that time in fourth grade when we all had to have class outside for a day while they brought in a professional cleaning crew. "We could really get in trouble for going through a staff-only door. Besides, there's so much more of the museum to see, like—"

But Harry cut me off.

"Aww, Lloyd never gets in trouble," he said, putting his arm around his best friend. "We have a whole system worked out. Anytime Lloyd is up to something sneaky, I stand watch. Then, when we get caught, I talk our way out of it while Lloyd gets away."

Harry smiled and pulled his pal closer. I don't think he realized that what he was describing was . . . Lloyd ditching Harry to take the blame. But the way Lloyd hugged Harry back, I don't think Lloyd saw it that way, either.

Sometimes you just have to admire when two perfectly paired people find each other in life.

"So you're saying you always get caught?" I asked, hoping to bring them to their senses.

"Yeah!" Harry said, like it was a good thing.

"Not at all!" Lloyd said at the exact same time.

Harry's smile dropped, and he looked to Lloyd, then back to me, then back to Lloyd again, before settling back on me.

"Not at all," Harry repeated after Lloyd. "We never ever get caught or in trouble. It'll be totally fine."

Zoe is my best friend. And my dog is my other best friend. You know who my other, *other* best friend is? The Rules.

"Guys, there's no way I'm breaking into an off-limits

part of the Smithsonian. Besides, it's probably just some maintenance room full of mops."

I crossed my arms and looked at my watch: Only one hour and fifty-five minutes left to do the packet questions. We were burning perfectly good museum time.

As I spoke, Lloyd started backing up toward the no-entry door. He faked a big yawn and stretched his arms out like he had just woken up.

"That's a bummer to hear, Hunter," Lloyd said, calling me by my last name like we were old pals (we weren't).

"The exhibits out here are so boring, and I'm still sleepy from that bus ride. Right, Harry?"

"Sure thing, Lloyd," Harry responded. "Bumpy trips always remind me of my mattress back home."

Lloyd was right next to the staff door now, his arms still stretching this way and that.

"You said it, Harry," Lloyd went on. "Why, I might need to take a nap . . . right . . . here."

Lloyd put his hands together under his chin, like he was a perfect angel resting on a pillow. Before I could stop him, he started to tip over toward the door. Then his eyes popped open again, and a devilish grin ruined his innocent facade.

"Oops, wouldn't want to fall and hurt myself."

Lloyd smoothly reached out his hands and pushed open the Staff Only door. Harry rushed in after, a goofy smile plastered on his face.

Lloyd waved me over, and I saw his hand move in slow

motion as my mind cycled through possible outcomes.

An alarm, super loud or totally silent, could go off at any second. Museum guards would swarm us, Mrs. McCormick would be contacted, and Harry, Lloyd, and I would probably be kicked out and maybe even sent home early.

(All things considered, the field trip ending before it really began might not have been the worst thing in the world.)

Or the hallway could lead to something really uninteresting, like a broom closet, or the locker room where museum staff change into their fancy blazers.

Or . . . the door could open up to a hidden part of the museum full of artifacts too priceless to even display behind security glass, in which case both museum guards AND probably the FBI would show up to escort us out in handcuffs.

Lloyd's hand sped back up, and he winked at me. In a decision I immediately knew I would regret, I quickly looked both ways and followed them beyond the staff door.

CHAPTER 4

As soon as the door shut behind us, I knew I'd made a huge mistake. "Innocent bystander" was out the window. But someone had to keep an eye on these two, right? And I was fairly certain I could throw them under the (proverbial) bus if we got caught.

"No alarm—we're in the clear, crew," Lloyd whispered.

"Aww yeah!" Harry responded, in the opposite of a whisper.

"It could be a silent alarm," I reminded them.

"As if a *silent* alarm matters," Lloyd responded. "No one would even hear it!"

"There might be cameras," I said, getting desperate. "Come on, guys—this is far enough. Let's get back to the museum hall and finish our assignment."

Lloyd ignored my pleas and edged his way down the hallway. From what I could see, it was empty, poorly lit, and totally nondescript. I figured it almost *definitely* led

to an air-conditioning control panel or something else boring, so I hoped Lloyd would come to his senses and give
up before we got caught. But that wasn't going to happen
until he saw for himself what was behind the forbidden
door.

"Quiet, gang," Lloyd said, snapping against the wall like he
was in a spy caper. Harry did the same, but I just rolled my
eyes and continued walking normally.

By this point, I was prepared to lie and claim we got lost
looking for the bathroom.

Before long, we came upon a turn in the hallway. Lloyd
held his hand up, signaling us to stop.

"I'm going to use a secret spy technique to check
around this corner for danger," Lloyd said.

I assumed he was going to try to angle a mirror or
other shiny surface to see at an angle without revealing too
much of himself, but Lloyd just ducked his entire head
around the corner and quickly pulled it back.

"Mixed news, my agile little ninjas," he said. "There *is* a
camera . . . but someone has already disabled it."

"How can you tell?" I asked. "You looked at it for half a
second. And if it is working, security probably flagged you
and are on their way here now."

Now Lloyd rolled his eyes, and then his entire head.

"I *told* you—secret spy technique," he responded once
his head came to a stop. "And I know what I saw. Someone
has covered the lens in spray paint."

"That means we're onto something extra cool!" Harry said, bouncing up and down in place.

I was past my limit with make-believe spy games. I marched past the boys to see for myself, fully expecting to find a broom closet or a service elevator. Only Lloyd was right—there *was* a security camera ahead of us in the hall-way, right above another door. And it *did* look like someone had sprayed black spray paint all over the lens in a hurry. It was still wet and dripping in some spots.

I turned back around to gather the boys and get out of there, but they walked right past me toward the unmarked door.

"What are you doing?" I whispered, now taking this side trip much more seriously. "We have to get out of here and tell security something is going on."

"You're totally right," Lloyd said, pushing open the door. "And security will be *so* grateful when we see for ourselves what's going on, so we can report it to them without missing any important details!"

I looked to Harry, hoping his sense of danger might have kicked in. But he just shrugged. I got the feeling Lloyd had put him in similar situations more than a few times over the course of their friendship.

Gritting my teeth, I followed the boys through the door, which opened on a staircase that went down into darkness. I didn't *want* to follow them, but I felt responsible for their bizarre, naive lives. But when I saw the darkness ahead of us, I put my foot down. One forbidden hallway, shame on me. Two forbidden hallways, shame on you. Two forbidden hallways *and* a creepy staircase? Shame on everyone and everything that led to this situation.

"Uh-uh, too much. We're going back the way we came," I insisted, holding open the door and waving my free arm frantically in that direction.

"Oh, I would, but I'm already sliding down the stairs," Lloyd said, scooting down the handrail. I could tell the handrail hadn't been polished or cleaned in ages because it actually took Lloyd a lot of effort to *pretend* he was sliding down it against his will. He basically had to pull his way along inch by inch, and I could see on his face that it wasn't as comfortable as expected. Not to mention that each landing had a pole at the end, so he had to get off one handrail and get back on the next one. It was . . . excruciating to watch.

Harry hurried alongside Lloyd, and I decided sticking with them was at least better than staying in a dark staircase by myself (but only by a little bit).

If this was to be my last day on Earth, I just hoped that everyone would know I died doing what I hate: putting up with total idiots.

The stairs went down three floors, which meant we must have been underneath the public part of the museum, completely off the map they give you when you walk in. As we approached the bottom, I could see light where the stairs opened up into another room.

Even after I begrudgingly went along with them, Lloyd kept up his sliding act all the way to the bottom, so it took us a good five minutes to reach the floor. At the bottom of the stairs, I finally saw where the light was coming from: a *huge* warehouse-like room full of crates stacked on top of crates. I could see some of the nearby boxes labeled with dinosaur names or ancient places like Mesopotamia.

"Harry, Lloyd—do you know what this place is?" I asked in awe, briefly forgetting how illegal the whole situation was.

Lloyd shook his head sadly and kicked at the ground in front of him.

"Yeah, my aunt shops at a place just like this," he replied. "You get a members-only card, but all you can buy are jumbo packs of toilet paper and huge bags of granola."

Lloyd looked disappointed and turned to walk back up the steps.

"This isn't a bulk grocery store, Lloyd," I explained. "This must be where the museum keeps all the things it can't display, just like you thought. Look at the labels on the crates!"

Harry squinted at a box that read STEGOSAURUS on the side, and I expected him to get really excited. Instead, he just scratched at his chin.

"If only we knew how to read Latin," he said with a sigh.

Reading comprehension was the least of our problems, though. Just then, a loud "crack!" echoed around the warehouse. All three of us ducked and hid behind the *Stegosaurus* crate.

"No fear, fellow agents," Lloyd said, attempting to take charge of the situation. "I'll use my patented spy technique to investigate."

I stuck my hand out to stop him. If the same person who took out the security camera made that noise, I didn't want to risk him seeing Lloyd's head popping out from around the corner of a dinosaur box.

"Let me handle it this time, 'agent,'" I said. I pulled out my phone and switched on camera mode. Then I stuck just the tip of it past the edge of the box, so I could see on the screen what the phone camera saw around the corner.

And what the phone showed me was trouble with a capital T: a security guard headed right in our direction.

Secret
Attack Plan
by Harry and Lloyd

CHAPTER 5

I yanked my phone back and made sure the sound and flashlight were turned off. Then I turned toward Harry and Lloyd and brought my finger to my lips to try to shush them.

"Ooh, charades?" Harry asked. "One word, huh? What does it start with?"

"Parlor games will have to wait, Harry," Lloyd said. "I think our new friend Tini has spotted an even *newer* friend."

We didn't have time for more of their back-and-forth, so I cupped my hands around both of their mouths and gave them the most serious glare I could muster.

(And yes, I did thoroughly sanitize my hands the next chance I got.)

We pressed ourselves against the crate as the tall, lanky figure walked past us. I held my breath, hoping he'd keep on walking, but he came to a stop about ten feet away. If he turned around, he'd be looking RIGHT at the three of us.

"Time is of the essence . . . Where is the crate?" the guard said. He was looking around the stacks and stacks of wooden boxes in front of him.

I glanced at Harry and Lloyd and saw that both were starting to fidget. I didn't think either was used to staying quiet for more than five seconds at a time.

"Aha!" the guard said. He hurried over toward a crate labeled MELEAGRIS, and for once Harry and I were on the same page because I had no idea what that word meant.

As we watched, the guard pulled a crowbar out from under his shirt and started prying away pieces of the wooden crate.

"Wow, being a security guard looks *awesome*," Harry whispered. If not for all the noise caused by the crate's destruction, the guard would have heard that for sure.

After a few more planks were broken off, the man pulled an object out of the crate.

"The Order thought we'd find you at the National Museum of American History, but I see that the fools in charge of these institutions had no idea of your true worth," he said, admiring . . . a stuffed turkey? "*Meleagris gallopavo . . .*"

"Ah, he's Italian," Lloyd whispered to me.

"He's not Italian," I whispered back, against my better instincts. "That must be the scientific name for—"

"The domestic turkey!" the man whispered, almost reverently. "But not just any domestic turkey . . ."

The turkey the man was holding looked like it had seen better days. I don't know how old it was, but it was missing half its feathers, the left wing was noticeably smaller than the right, and one of its glass eyes was dangling from the socket. No wonder the museum kept it boxed up three stories underground.

Things got weirder almost immediately (a pattern you tend to notice when Harry and Lloyd are involved). As we watched, the guard pulled open the dusty turkey's beak and reached his forearm into the bird's throat.

Next to me, I heard a quiet whistling noise that quickly picked up in volume. The smell hit me a moment later, and Harry blushed as I recognized what had just happened.

"Sorry," he mouthed to me. "I had dairy for lunch."

Then I heard a sniffing noise, and the guard whipped his head toward us. I made direct eye contact with the strange man whose arm was stuck down a taxidermy turkey's neck.

"What are you doing here?" the man asked, as if we were the most preposterous thing about the situation.

At this point, I was pretty sure he wasn't an actual museum guard, but I wasn't going to take any chances with a man sporting a crowbar and a stuffed turkey.

"We got lost looking for the rest of our class," I said. "We don't want anything to do with your . . . turkey troubles." As I spoke, I realized the guy looked familiar, but I couldn't place him right away.

The mysterious man waved his arm around, the turkey still engulfing his right hand.

"This is no ordinary turkey, you interlopers," he growled. "This fine fowl was once the personal companion of Benjamin Franklin, one of this country's most legendary founders."

Apologies to Ben Franklin, then, because the man's movements caused the brittle neck of the turkey to split in two.

Harry dove to catch the remainder of the bird as if it might be wounded by the fall. Sorry, Harry—that bird was already well past saving.

"Caught it!" Harry said as he landed hard on his stomach. "Ooh, and look, there's something sticking out of your bird, mister."

Harry was right—there was a rolled-up cylinder of paper poking out of the turkey where the neck used to attach. Clearly, this was what the man was digging for.

The man in the guard outfit lunged for the paper, trying to take it out of Harry's hands, but Harry stepped back just in time.

"Hey, you could have just asked!" Harry said, wagging his finger at the man. "It's not polite to *grab* things."

The man straightened out his big bushy mustache and took a deep breath.

"Wrestling with children is . . . beneath me," he said, trying to compose himself.

Then it hit me . . . I knew why I recognized this guy! A tall kind of sweaty man with a mustache — it was the stranger who'd stepped on Harry's assignment packet in the rotunda! He told me to forget his face, but who could forget a face like that?

"Harry, get back!" I shouted. "This man isn't a guard."

"That's all I needed to hear," Lloyd said from behind me. "Consider the cavalry . . . called." I turned around to see that Lloyd had his hand on the fire alarm.

"WEEYOOWEEYOOWEEYOO" started blaring all around us, and the mustache man covered his ears to block it out.

"Enough of this!" he said, dropping the crowbar with a loud "CLANG." "Reginald California will not be made a fool of!" He sprinted headlong toward Harry, who was still holding the turkey body and the roll of paper within it.

Harry panicked and ran, too . . . only he ran right toward the charging stranger instead of away from him. They collided in a cloud of flying feathers, as mustache met very, very old bird.

The man — apparently named Reginald California, although that's not the sort of name I'd announce proudly if it were mine — slapped his hands around the floor in search of the secret scroll. The dust from the collision was still in his eyes and blocking his view. He grabbed the rolled-up papers nearest to him and stomped away, shouting after us as he went.

"Stay out of my way, you meddling brats!" he said,

coughing out dust. "The Order of the Snood doesn't take kindly to interference!"

With the fire alarm still echoing through the warehouse, the bizarre man with the sweaty mustache disappeared into the shadows.

I rushed over to help Harry and make sure he wasn't hurt, when I saw that the collision had caused him to spill the contents of his backpack. While Harry shook out his musty hair, I bent down to grab his assignment book for him.

Only . . . it wasn't his rolled-up question packet — it was whatever strange scroll had been tucked inside that turkey's neck!

CHAPTER 6

"Lloyd, cut it out, he's gone already," Harry said as he rubbed the last of the dirt out of his eyes.

On cue, the "fire alarm" stopped as quickly as it had started.

"Wait a minute," I said. "That terrible sound was *you* the whole time? You didn't really trigger the alarm?"

Lloyd bowed, taking my shock as high praise.

"With hours and hours of practice, you can sound like almost any annoying sound," he said proudly.

"Then that means there aren't any real guards on their way to help us, either, right?" I said, suddenly nervous. I clutched the strange roll of paper to my chest and looked around to make sure this Reginald California guy wasn't coming back for it.

"Nah, I just wanted to scare that guy away so we could keep that awesome stuffed turkey to ourselves," Lloyd said. "But now it's totally busted. What a waste of a good bird."

Harry was still picking feathers out of his hair as Lloyd said this.

"I don't think he was after the turkey," I said, carefully unrolling the paper. "I think he was after *this*."

I held up the weathered roll of parchment so the boys could see it, too. The warehouse didn't have great lighting, and the ink on the paper had faded over the years, but it didn't take me long to realize I was looking at a map that more or less matched the National Mall and the various museums and monuments located along it.

There were strange symbols on different parts of the map, which seemed to correspond to different parts of a bird: the beak, the foot, the wing. And each symbol overlapped with a building.

Lloyd grabbed the delicate paper right out of my hands.

"Tini, Harry, do you know what this means?" he said, holding it up toward the nearest light for a better look. "Secret treasure map! Let's *go*!"

"Hold up," I said, trying to be the voice of reason. Lloyd was already halfway up the first flight of stairs, studying the map in his hand and barely listening to me. "We can't just take museum property. And we can't go wandering around the National Mall on our own—Mrs. McCormick made it very clear that we're *not* to leave the museum."

Lloyd's eyes lit up.

"National Mall? Oh, thank goodness, I've been dying for a

pretzel and a nice cold drink of artificially flavored high-fructose corn syrup," he said.

"It's not *that* kind of mall," I corrected him. "That's what this area of D.C. with the museums and the monuments is called."

Harry looked over Lloyd's shoulder at the map.

"Oh yeah," he said, "I can see little drawings of the big pointy statue and that man sitting in the chair and stuff."

(In case you missed it, that was Harry's understated way of referring to the Washington Monument and the Lincoln Memorial, respectively.)

"But what's with all the bird stuff?" he added.

"Harry, good buddy, isn't it obvious?" Lloyd responded. I didn't think *anything* about this situation was obvious, so I was eager to hear Lloyd's version of what was going on.

"The bird symbols are clues leading us across the map, which clearly ends at"—Lloyd stuck his arms out and made a jerky flapping motion, like he was a bird that couldn't quite take off—"a stockpile of golden turkey eggs, just like in 'The Turkey That Laid All Those Golden Eggs'!"

"Don't you think you're jumping to a few conclusions here, Lloyd?" I asked. "Also, the story is 'The Goose That Laid the Golden Egg.'" Also—that story is totally made up! It's just a symbolic fable."

Lloyd just kept trotting up the stairs, a grin on his face.

"I'm not jumping to conclusions at all, Tini Hunter. Why else would this map be hidden *inside* a stuffed turkey and

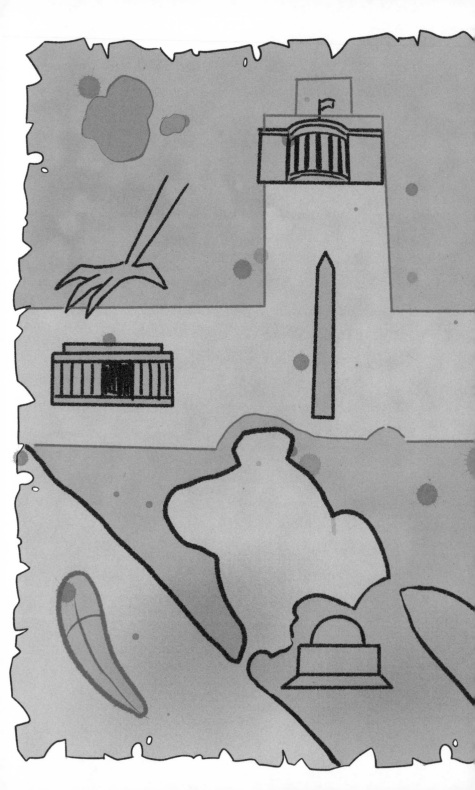

have gold lettering and turkey drawings all over it? The cymbal dism couldn't be stronger—to find the turkeys, you must *become* the turkey. And then the rich, delicious reward of golden eggs awaits us."

Harry nodded like this made perfect sense. I couldn't very well stay in the storage basement alone, so up we went, back to the empty hallway and the Staff Only door we never should have opened in the first place.

Part of me expected to open it and be met with a dozen guards in body armor, but when we cracked it a few inches to see the museum floor, no one was even looking in our direction. We slipped out as easily as we had snuck in, and I immediately started looking around for Mrs. McCormick.

"This way, my doubtful pal," Lloyd said, waving me over toward an exit.

"I told you—we can't just leave on our own," I shot back. I saw that there was a museum staffer standing by the exit door, anyway, which gave me a glimmer of hope that she could radio in three wayward kids and get someone to locate our chaperones before Lloyd and Harry got loose.

"Hello, children," she said as the boys approached her. The staffer was a kind-looking older woman who seemed like she genuinely enjoyed her job at the museum. "Can I help you today?"

"Yes, we're looking for our—" I started, but Lloyd cut me off.

"Actually," he said, pulling out his crumpled-up question packet. "Our teacher told us to find some information here and we're having a hard time. Maybe you can help?"

I didn't like where this was going.

"Oh, of course," the woman said. "I'd be happy to point you in the direction of the right exhibits."

Lloyd licked his finger and turned one of the pages.

"First question: What's the square root of 7,659,403?"

The volunteer frowned, and I could tell she wanted to say something like, *Oh, bless your heart*, which is what older people say to kids when they can't find a nice way to say, *Wow, you aren't very bright.*

"Ah, we don't really cover math here at the Smithsonia—"

Lloyd flipped to another page and cut her off.

"Got it, got it, maybe this one, then. What was the highest grossing movie of the year in 1994?"

This poor woman.

"Well, that's really more of a *trivia* question than—"

Lloyd flipped the page again. As he did so, he winked at Harry and tilted his head toward the exit door.

"Sure, sure. Here we go, I *know* you'll know this one: What did my aunt Colleen bring to the Christmas family potluck last summer?"

Harry had moved to the exit door now and had his hands ready to push it open. I should have intervened, but I was glued to Lloyd's bizarre method of outsmarting the museum employee.

"Let me just get you a map of the museum," the staffer said, admitting defeat. "Maybe you'll find some of the answers you're looking for on a . . . *self-guided* tour."

As soon as the staffer turned toward the information

desk, Harry and Lloyd were out the door. About two seconds later, I followed them.

I know, I know. Why did I go with them instead of tracking down an adult whom they couldn't confuse into submission? The answer is simple.

Because when I turned around, Reginald California was passing the information kiosk and heading right for us!

To my esteemed fellows
in the Order of the Snood,

Our intel regarding Benjamin Franklin's
codex was correct—as Brother ████████
surmised from his research, one of our
ancestors in the Order of the Snood hid it
within Franklin's prized turkey's gullet
(with all due respect to the turkey,
knowing Franklin's fondness for the fowl).
It is my grave dishonor to report, however,
that the map detailing the final steps
toward Franklin's cache, which we have
sought after for ████████ years, spending
████████ and sacrificing ████████ in
our quest, was intercepted by cunning and
sinister enemy agents, no doubt deployed by
████████ in the ongoing crusade against
our righteous cause. Have no fear, my dear
brothers—your trusted fellow in arms
Reginald J. California is in pursuit of the
dastardly scoundrels. I have paused only
long enough to compose and send this
missive, which will self-destruct, as all
of our top secret correspondences do,
within moments of your eyes taking in its
final lines.

Yours forever in the
bond of the Snood,
Reginald California

CHAPTER 7

"Move, go, go, go!" I urged the boys as we made our way through the crowd outside the Smithsonian.

Lloyd pumped his fist.

"Aww yeah, Tini is finally along for the adventure!"

"I am *not*," I responded. "I just don't want the turkey guy catching up with us now that he's realized we have that map."

I looked over my shoulder while we pushed through vacationers standing around gawking at the sights. Through the glass of the museum exit door, I could see this Reginald California—a name I will never get used to saying with a straight face—arguing with the kind museum staffer Lloyd had confused. Reginald had ditched whatever fake guard outfit he was wearing and was back in his trench coat, which was definitely too warm for the late-spring D.C. weather.

"Let's just get somewhere discreet so we can think this over and make a safe decision!"

One of my favorite things about being best friends with Zoey is that we always know what the other is going to do before we do it, like we have a telepathic link.

Unfortunately, Lloyd, Harry, and I *don't* have that.

I hurried onward, trying to keep one eye on the direction we came from in case Mr. California was following us. When I turned back ahead, Harry and Lloyd were nowhere to be found.

I paused to catch my breath and scan the faces around me. I saw a lot of sunburned dads, moms with fanny packs, and screaming kids, but no sixth-grade Tini-terrorizers.

"Say cheese!" I overheard in a recognizably grating voice.

Twenty feet away from me, I spotted Lloyd holding up an expensive-looking camera as a large family of six posed for a photo on the mall.

Scratch that—a family of five, along with Harry, who had his arm wrapped around the grandpa like they were old pals.

"Harry, Lloyd, what are you doing?" I whisper-shouted. "Do you know these people?"

"Nah, just being a good citizen," Lloyd responded. He kept clicking away at the camera, giving the family dozens of options to choose from (and I'm sure only about half of them had Lloyd's thumb in the frame).

"Well, wrap it up," I growled. "We're kind of in a hurry, in case you forgot."

Lloyd snapped a few more photos, then handed the camera back to the mom of the group.

"Sorry about my *rude* friend," he said. "Hope we got some good ones!"

"Don't you worry none, son," the woman replied in a thick Southern accent. "We appreciate y'all helpin' us out."

I tapped my foot impatiently as Lloyd made his way over to where I was standing. The family turned in the other direction to continue their vacation . . . along with the new straggler they had picked up.

"Harry, come on," I commanded.

Harry slapped his forehead. "Oops, my bad!" He waved goodbye to his new "family" and rejoined Lloyd and me. The Mall was busy enough that I was a little less nervous about Reginald spotting us, but I still wanted to get somewhere more secure.

I spotted a sculpture garden full of abstract art—plenty of weird shapes to hide behind.

On our way over to a big pile of metal squares and rectangles designated "art," Lloyd grabbed the map out of Harry's backpack and checked it against our surroundings.

"Wait just a single turkey-gobbling moment . . ." he said, looking down at the paper and back up at the building next to the sculpture garden. "That building over there is full of planes and spaceships, and it's got a wing symbol marking it on our map. Onward, intrepid fliers!"

"Aren't you even a little bit concerned about the strange man *chasing us around* to steal this map back?" I asked, hoping Lloyd would slow down and think things through for even one second. "Or how much trouble we'll get in when Mrs. McCormick finds out about all this?!"

"Not in the least," Lloyd replied. "Mrs. M. *loves* me. And what kind of secret race-against-time treasure-map adventure would this be without a villain hot on our heels? Especially one with such an *awesome* name."

Lloyd made a sharp turn *away* from the quiet, safe sculpture garden toward the National Air and Space Museum.

"Oh no, you're not dragging me into another museum where you can break the rules and steal weird hidden artifacts," I said, earning a strange look from a passing tourist.

"Well, we probably shouldn't stay here," Harry said, pointing behind me.

I hadn't spotted Reginald California, but Harry sure did. Despite the mustache, this strange man was pretty good at blending into the crowd. Luckily for us, he was speed-walking instead of running—likely to avoid attracting any attention. He may have some weird ideas about turkeys, but this guy was no fool.

Lloyd looked pleased to see our pursuer, if only because it made it more likely I'd go along with his plan.

"What do you say, Tini Hunter? Want to stay and talk it out, or shall we explore the wonders of air and space?"

Lloyd didn't see me roll my eyes because I was already hurrying toward the National Air and Space Museum. I couldn't predict what Reginald would do to get that map back, but I was betting that he wouldn't want to be seen chasing children across the National Mall. If we could make it inside the museum before he caught up with us, maybe that would buy us some time.

We sprinted over to the museum and ran right into a problem: There was a line to get inside that stretched at least a hundred people deep. I turned around and saw that Reginald was still speed-walking right for us with Harry's crumpled-up assignment packet in his hand.

"This is no good," I said, looking around for another place to run. "We're sitting ducks in this line."

"Harry, Lloyd, git over here!" someone shouted from closer to the museum entrance. The voice was friendly and had a Southern accent. I squinted against the midday sun and recognized . . . the family Lloyd and Harry had taken photos with a few minutes before! They were standing in a much *shorter* line at another door to the museum.

"Oh, hey, Ernie!" Harry said.

I have to admit this about the boys: They sure do leave lasting impressions on people.

Ernie, the apparent grandpa of this vacationing clan, waved us over. I glanced back one more time to see the man with the mustache getting closer through the crowd.

"We got this here priority pass," Ernie explained, displaying a printed-out ticket. "It's good for anyone in our party. Why don't y'all walk in with us so you don't gotta stand out here in the sun?"

"Why, that's mighty nice of y'all," Harry replied, mimicking Ernie's Southern twang.

Within moments, a staff member scanned Ernie's pass and waved all of us inside the National Air and Space Museum, no waiting in line required. Harry and Lloyd made small talk with the family—all of it in their horrible versions of Southern accents—and then the friendly group went along their way.

"And that," Lloyd said, turning to face me, "is why it always pays to be friendly."

I wasn't a fan of learning life lessons from these two, but I couldn't argue with the results. Especially when I turned around and saw Reginald California trying to sweet-talk his way into the priority entrance. After a brief argument with the entrance staffer, who was not budging, he trudged over to the general admissions line. Based on how slowly it was moving, I figured we had at least fifteen or twenty minutes to sort out a plan before he was on our trail again.

I let out a sigh of relief, but the relief didn't last long. When I turned back to Harry and Lloyd, I saw their eyes light up at the sight of all the air- and spacecraft suspended above us. I could already see the gears of chaos spinning in their heads.

CHAPTER 8

"I'm warning you both right now: If you try to step one single foot in any of these jets, planes, or space shuttles, I will make sure you are grounded—permanently."

If I had learned anything from my time with Harry and Lloyd, it was that they subscribe to the "ask forgiveness, not permission" school of making wild decisions. I wanted them to know up front that I never forgive and I *never* permit.

Lloyd ignored me and took the map out of Harry's backpack again. The way Lloyd relied on Harry carting things around was starting to remind me of a pack mule. Lloyd unfolded it and ran his finger across the cracked surface until he found the wing symbol drawn over the building where the Air and Space Museum now stands.

"As enticing as these fine flying machines are," Lloyd said, "we're looking for something related to wings, according to the map."

Harry started pointing to every plane he could see around him.

(Since this is a museum dedicated to flight, there were a *lot* of planes around him.)

"Ooh, there's a wing, Lloyd," he said. "And there, too. And hey, that plane has *four* of them!"

"Harry is right," I said. The words felt wrong in my mouth. "Almost everything in this museum has wings of some sort. And besides, we don't know what that map means or what the symbols correspond to."

Lloyd looked at me with pity.

"Sweet, simple Tini—this map has turkey drawings in each corner, shiny gold lettering, and bird signs all over it. I think I know a puzzle map leading to a paradise full of golden-egg-laying turkeys when I see one."

I tried to explain everything wrong with that sentence, but Lloyd walked away before I could get a word out. Harry and I exchanged confused glances and then followed.

Lloyd made a beeline toward the nearest museum employee. I quickly checked to make sure that he didn't have a big suspicious mustache—all clear.

"Excuse me," Lloyd said, holding the map behind his back, where the staffer couldn't see it. "I'm looking for something very . . . specific."

"And what might that be, young man?" the employee asked. I was crossing my fingers that Lloyd wasn't going to talk this guy in circles like he did to the poor woman at the other museum.

"I'm looking for something with *feathers*," Lloyd said.

The employee let out a small laugh. *Good*, I thought—maybe he'd squash Lloyd's fantasy of a secret golden turkey sanctuary or whatever he had convinced himself waited on the other side of that map.

"I think you've got us confused with the Museum of Natural History," the staffer said. "Our jets and shuttles don't have any—" He paused for a second, stroking his chin. "Actually, we do have *one* exhibit with feathers. The last hallway on the left, past the vending machine and the infant changing room. The Hall of Failed Flying Inventions."

Lloyd gave the man an exaggerated bow of thanks and then turned around to stick his tongue out at me.

We made our way through the museum, following the employee's directions. By the time we reached the hallway he mentioned, the crowds had thinned out. It seemed like this section was a little less popular than the other exhibits.

I quickly understood why: The Hall of Failed Flying Inventions was pretty small and only had a handful of half-empty glass display cases. The bulb in one of them was flickering, making the place feel like the world's most pathetic dance party, and the sign overhead actually read HA OF FA LED FLYI G MACHIN S because some of the letters had fallen off and no one had bothered to fix it.

Lloyd's and Harry's eyes lit up.

"The map was right!" Lloyd said, sprinting over to the last display case in the corner. Inside was a contraption that looked like a life-sized bird puppet that had been hollowed out. I wiped a thick layer of dust off the plaque and was shocked at what I read:

BENJAMIN FRANKLIN'S PROTOTYPE PERSONAL FLYING SUIT, 1751

Reginald California had been going on about that wonky stuffed turkey having belonged to Ben Franklin. I was still pretty certain Lloyd's hopes and dreams of golden turkey eggs weren't real, but it seemed like the map we took certainly pointed to *something* going on here.

Lloyd put both hands on the glass, admiring the ridiculous suit within as if *it* were made of gold instead of musty feathers. I would have worried about him tripping an alarm, but I didn't think the museum paid to extend security to this neglected wing.

"You know what this means?" Lloyd asked.

"Ben Franklin didn't understand the laws of physics?" I responded. "This is the Hall of *Failed* Flying Machines, after all."

Lloyd slowly turned around, his grin practically reaching the tips of his protruding ears.

"Time to soar, my friends," Lloyd answered.

Oh no, I thought to myself. *They're going to try to wear this dumb bird suit.*

Plan for bird soot

CHAPTER 9

"Lemme put it on first, Lloyd, please!" Harry whined. He was standing next to Lloyd at the glass case containing the feather-clad flying suit. Harry's face was smooshed against the glass, which I'm sure hadn't been cleaned since before any of us were born.

Lloyd stretched out one hand toward his friend's face, and dramatically turned his own head in the other direction.

"If only I could, Harry," Lloyd said. "I would love nothing more than to see my best friend take to the skies in the freedom of flight, but how could I ever forgive myself?"

Harry looked confused.

(I didn't blame him.)

"Forgive yourself?" he asked.

Lloyd put his hand to his chest, pretending to be shocked.

"Of course—this suit is a phonogram, after all," he responded.

"You mean a *prototype*, and a failed one, at that," I corrected. "From, like, three hundred years ago. And it's now museum property. Don't forget about that." They pretended not to hear me.

"If you were to wear it first and anything malfunctioned, I couldn't live with myself!" Lloyd said. He pretended to wipe a tear away from his eye. Let's just say it wasn't a performance that would earn any standing ovations in drama class, but Harry seemed moved. He wiped away an *actual* tear and gave Lloyd a big hug.

"Aww, Lloyd," Harry said, sniffling. "I'm so lucky to have a friend like you who's always looking out for me."

Lloyd returned the hug for a moment, then pushed Harry back to arm's length.

"That's right, buddy of mine," Lloyd said. "And now *you* can look out for *me* by creating a distraction while I free this suit from its glass prison."

Before I could object to the craziness Lloyd proposed, my phone vibrated in my pocket. I pulled it out to see . . . BFF ZOEY on the screen?

I took a deep breath before answering, so Zoey wouldn't notice how relieved I was to see her name pop up.

"Oh . . . hey," I said, trying to play it cool. "I thought we, like, weren't talking right now or whatever."

"We're not," she responded. "But one of the other kids saw you and your weirdo new friends leave the museum, and now Mrs. McCormick is freaking out."

84

"They're not my—" I started to say, and then I caught myself. I weighed my options:

Do I try to explain everything as quickly as possible (probably leaving out some of the stranger turkey-related details) and hope that Mrs. McCormick rushes over here and shuts this whole mess down?

Or do I spin . . . maybe bend the truth a little, so I can be the responsible one and solve this mess on my own? (A mess that may or may not have gotten worse because I made a few less-than-responsible decisions.)

"Uh, Earth to Tini? Are you still there?" I heard through the phone's speaker. I was about to respond when I heard a scream and then a collective gasp behind me, coming from the main hall of the museum.

When I looked around for Harry and Lloyd, only Lloyd was still there, standing next to the case containing the bird suit, doing his best to suppress a giggle.

I put my hand over the phone so Zoey couldn't hear me, and angrily whispered at Lloyd.

"Where did Harry go? We have to stick together!"

"Hmm, couldn't say for sure," he responded. "I'd follow the roar of the crowd, if I were you." I gave him a stare that could freeze a rhino in its tracks.

"Sorry, Zoey," I said, sprinting toward the noises. "Tell Mrs. McCormick I've got everything under control. Almost *definitely* under control."

"Wait, Tini—" is all that she managed to get out before

I hung up on her and pocketed my phone again. When I turned the corner into the main hall, I saw a crowd gathered below the big space shuttle suspended from the ceiling.

"Get down from there, kid!" a guard shouted from my left.

I joined the crowd in craning my neck up toward the rafters and found . . . Harry walking along the shuttle's wing!

"I'm going on a space walk!" he yelled down at us. Harry had both arms stuck out to the side, wobbling as he tried to keep his balance. The shuttle was easily thirty feet off the ground, if not more. If he tipped too far left or too far right, Harry Dunne was done for.

"Harry!" I shouted, trying to get his attention over the concerned mumbles of the crowd. "How did you even get up there?!"

Harry spotted me in the crowd and waved. I was afraid the motion was going to send him right over the side of the shuttle.

"Oh, hey, Tini! Don't worry about me. I'm just the distraction!" Then he gave a big, obvious wink in my direction.

Now you understand why Lloyd and Harry usually get caught.

There were at least forty or fifty shocked museum guests standing below the shuttle now, along with a handful of staffers and guards on walkie-talkies, trying to radio for help.

It's not like there was a ladder or anything leading to the shuttle, so I still to this day have no idea how Harry got up there, and I didn't have a clue then how he was going to get down. All I could do was watch as he teetered back and forth, and hope that he and Lloyd had thought things through beyond just the distraction part of their harebrained scheme.

And yes, I realize that that was asking for a lot from those two.

Just then, someone shouted and pointed to the jet plane next to the space shuttle. I looked over and saw that a police officer had climbed onto the wing and was reaching out for Harry.

What a relief, I thought—for the first time that day, a helpful adult had arrived in a timely fashion!

"Harry, go toward the officer!" I shouted. "You've distracted enough! We have to get you down from there!"

"Okay, Tini, if you say so!"

Harry started wobbling his way toward the officer's outstretched arms. That's when I noticed the big bushy mustache below the "officer's" mirrored sunglasses.

CHAPTER 10

"Harry, get *away* from the officer!" I yelled.

Harry stopped in his tracks, a confused look on his face. The space shuttle swayed under his feet.

"But you just said—"

"I know what I said!" I shouted. The tourists and staffers around me cast weird looks in my direction. They were fooled by Reginald's expert disguise, but I knew better. "Take a closer look—that's no police officer!"

Harry squinted at Reginald, who leapt off the jet plane, landing on the shuttle wing just a few feet from Harry. The whole shuttle rocked back and forth, and the crowd around me scattered, afraid of what might happen if the shuttle got to rocking *too* hard.

"Give me the map, boy!" Reginald growled. He ripped off his mirrored sunglasses, and I could see the anger in his eyes from where I was standing on the ground.

Harry pulled the backpack around to the front of his body and clutched it tight against his chest.

"Uh-uh, no way," he said. "Maybe if you had asked nicely earlier, but you're way too much of a meanie head now. You don't deserve to find the golden eggs."

"Golden eggs . . . ? You know nothing of the Order of the Snood!" Reginald shouted, taking another big step forward. Harry edged backward, but he was quickly running out of wing to stand on.

I looked around, hoping to magically find an exhibit on airbags or trampolines, but no such luck.

"That map doesn't lead to some simple, gaudy treasure," Reginald said, closing the gap between him and Harry. "It holds the key to unlocking some of this country's most closely guarded secrets!"

"That's not what my friend Lloyd said!" Harry barked back.

"And where is that friend of yours now, boy?" Reginald hissed, still advancing. "I don't see him here by your side when you need him most."

Harry backed up again; only, there was no shuttle left for him to stand on. I watched helplessly as the heel of his beat-up old boots slid off the edge of the ship. Harry could only wobble back and forth, attempting to keep his balance.

"Uh-oh!" Harry said, the understatement of the century. With one more wobble, he tipped over the side, and I instinctively covered my eyes to avoid watching him ker-splat on the museum floor.

Only, I didn't hear a thump—I heard a "WHOOSH"!

I looked up and saw . . . Lloyd, dressed in the ridiculous feather-covered flying suit! He flew past the wing of the shuttle and caught Harry with perfect timing.

"I've got ya, buddy!" Lloyd said, the wind whipping the dusty feathers around his face. "Now hang on tight because I haven't learned how to steer this thing yet!"

Lloyd wasn't kidding—he swerved left, right, up, and down like a feather duster in a tornado. Harry clung to the back of the suit for dear life as they narrowly dodged space capsules, fighter jets, and old-timey biplanes displayed around the museum's massive hangar. Each time they rushed by me, Harry's face looked greener and greener.

I kept covering my eyes with my hands, sure that they were going to make like a bird hitting a glass window any second. But once the initial shock wore off, my brain finally caught up to what was happening and realized . . . *there's no way Lloyd actually got that suit to fly.*

Sure enough, when I forced myself to look up, I could see that Lloyd had gotten hooked on one of the wires hanging from the ceiling. All of Reginald's stomping on the shuttle must have shaken one loose, and the shuttle's loss was Lloyd and Harry's gain. Without that stroke of luck, the boys really would have been a smear of *yuck.*

"Get down here, you disrespectful cads!" Reginald shouted. While I was busy watching Harry and Lloyd spin in fixed circles around the National Air and Space Museum, Reginald had crawled down off the space shuttle and was now running after the boys, trying to grab them—and the map—each time their rotation dipped them within his reach.

The rest of the museum was in pure chaos mode, with guests, staffers, and guards all equally clueless about the ridiculous situation. I'm pretty sure some of the vacationing tourists thought this was all part of a planned show, which would be asking a lot of a museum with free admission.

While Reginald chased them around in circles, I looked for the exit with the widest doors. I darted over to a set of double doors and swung them wide. The alarm sounded, but at that point, nothing was going to make the situation crazier than it already was.

"Harry, unhook the cable when I tell you to!" I shouted, my hands cupped around my mouth so he could hear me over the noise.

"What cable?" Lloyd yelled back. "We're *flying*!"

Harry, whose stomach was definitely feeling all the spinning in circles, caught my eye and nodded solemnly.

As I watched for the right moment, Reginald snapped toward my direction and charged at me with a snarl on his face. He was fast, but I was counting on the feathered fools being faster.

"Now!" I shouted, eyeballing the angle and velocity to the best of my sixth-grade ability. Harry unhooked the cable, and for a brief, unbelievable moment, the boys soared through the open air . . . with all the grace of . . . well, with absolutely no grace at all, to be honest — but plenty of screaming. The desperate move worked, though: Lloyd swooped right out the open doors, Harry still clinging desperately to his back. I darted out the doors myself and then slammed them shut as fast as I could.

Ker-SPLAT!

Reginald ran face-first into the door and left a smear of sweat as he slid down the glass. I expected the boys to crash right outside the museum, but the surprised oohs and aahs I could hear around me – and the fact that a big pile of feathers was nowhere in sight – told me Lloyd and Harry had made it a good distance away from the museum before landing.

The slammed doors wouldn't slow Reginald down for long, but it gave me enough of a head start to follow the trail of old dusty feathers scattered around and find out where Harry and Lloyd went from high-flying turkeys to flightless birds.

CHAPTER 11

You might think a sixth grader in a feathered flying suit gliding across the National Mall would be a big security concern, but apparently the sight of Lloyd and Harry in the sky was so ridiculous, a lot of people simply couldn't process it.

"Aliens!" one man started shouting. "I knew they were real! You mocked me for my tinfoil hat, but who's laughing now?!" His ravings drew a crowd of their own, and soon the vacationing horde was arguing among themselves over whether or not extraterrestrials exist.

Meanwhile, I spotted Lloyd and Harry making one last, sad loop before crash-landing in the branches of a tree off to the far side of the museum. Thanks to the man screaming about aliens, no one seemed to notice the final seconds of their time in the sky.

I sprinted over to the tree that caught their fall and saw that Lloyd was tangled in the branches about ten feet

off the ground, while Harry sat at the base of the tree rubbing his head.

"Harry, Lloyd—I'm so glad you guys are okay!" I said.
And I meant it—these two were trouble, but I was relieved
nothing seemed to be broken beyond the likely priceless
artifact Lloyd had stolen from the museum.

"Okay?!" Harry shouted. "I'm not okay! I just flew
through the air, and it wasn't awesome *at all*. I feel seasick,
but from the sky!"

"At least you landed on your head," Lloyd snarked down
at his friend. "I banged my *knee* on a branch coming in,
Harry."

Harry stood up and kicked the base of the tree.

"Ask me if I care, Lloyd!"

"Do you ca—"

"No, Lloyd, *I don't*! I don't care!"

Now it was my turn to step in and try to intervene.
With Reginald California hot on our trail and the distinct
chance that the National Guard's radar had spotted two
unidentified flying boZos, we didn't have time for a friend
fight.

"C'mon, boys—there's no reason to argue with each
other. We've already got a mustached lunatic chasing us."

"Exactly," Harry said, giving the tree another good kick.
"And thanks to Lloyd, that California guy almost got me! I
fell off the wing of a *space shuttle*, Lloyd—and I can't
breathe in space!"

I know that Zoey and I had just had a big fight and weren't talking to each other, but something about seeing Harry and Lloyd go at it just broke my heart. For as goofy as they each are, they just make total sense together as best friends. How many people are lucky enough to find a buddy on the exact same wavelength of weird as they are?

"Okay, let's take a deep breath," I said. "Harry, you're right—Lloyd did put a lot of the risk on you as a decoy. And, Lloyd, Harry deserves an apology because it sounds like this isn't the *first* time you've made him be the distraction while you carried out some harebrained scheme."

Harry looked up at Lloyd with an honest, innocent frown on his face. Lloyd started to frown, too, then sharply turned his head away.

"And, Harry, you have to give Lloyd some credit. Yes, he let you get stuck on a wing of a space shuttle with a strange man trying to capture you, *but* Lloyd showed up when it mattered and literally caught you before you could fall. That's the sign of a good friend."

Now Harry looked away in a huff.

As he did so, the branch holding up Lloyd made a loud "CREEEEAAAAAAK" noise and then, "SNAP," broke in half! Without thinking, Harry moved to catch Lloyd.

I wouldn't say it was an *entirely* successful save since they both ended up flat on the ground, but Harry's quick thinking broke Lloyd's fall—and it seemed like no bones were broken in the process.

"Harry, you saved my life!" Lloyd exclaimed.

"Well, of course I did, Lloyd," Harry replied. "You're my best friend."

"Now that you're even, can we get out of here?" I chimed in. "Reginald California is going to catch up with us if we stay this close to the museum. He can probably follow your trail of feathers."

Lloyd untangled himself from Harry and stood up, spreading the wings of the flying suit wide. Or what was left of the wings, anyway—between the flight in the museum, the first crash landing, and the second crash landing, there wasn't much you could still reasonably call a suit.

"Yeah, about that . . ." Lloyd said. "I don't think this birdie is taking to the clear blue skies again."

I tried not to think about the fact that we'd stolen something Ben Franklin created three hundred years ago and trashed it in a tree.

Lloyd gave the suit one last pitiful flap, which was more than it could handle. As he lifted his arms, the backpack contraption split right in half, and what was left of the suit fell to pieces around him—including one piece that glimmered in the light.

"Ooh, shiny," Harry said, fishing the object out of a pile of old feathers and broken wood.

"A turkey foot!" Lloyd shouted, and he wasn't wrong. One side of the small metal object Harry was holding was a sculpted turkey foot. But the other side was . . .

"A key!" I said.

Harry turned it this way and that, examining both sides.

"Oh yeah, a key *and* a turkey's foot. What will they think of next?"

"Harry, get the map out of your backpack," I ordered. Harry wobbled to his feet and fished the crumpled-up parchment from his bag. This scroll had seemingly survived for decades in the neck of a stuffed turkey, but an hour in Harry's bag had already done a number on it.

"I knew it!" I said, pointing to an icon of a bird's foot on the map. "The wing symbol matched up with the bird suit we found in the Air and Space Museum. And if we backtrack, there's a drawing of a turkey's neck wattles over at the Smithsonian."

"So where's the foot taking us, Captain Tini?" Lloyd asked. As I excitedly looked around the map for the symbol of the foot, I realized these two doofuses had gotten me hooked into their little scavenger hunt.

(Don't judge me—the other option was trying to explain Reginald California to the authorities. It was easier to follow the clues at this point.)

"Here we go—the turkey's foot is all the way across the Mall at the Lincoln Memorial," I said, spotting the mark on the map. "C'mon, we've got to hurry!"

"Aww yeah!" Lloyd and Harry said in unison.

"But first," Lloyd said, pointing in the opposite direction of the Lincoln Memorial, "time for some street food!"

CHAPTER 12

"Lloyd, you can't be serious!" I said.

"Oh, Tini," he replied. "I never, ever joke about street food."

I looked to Harry for help, but I could hear his stomach growling. It was a lost cause.

"I *am* pretty hungry," Harry admitted, looking down at the source of the gurgling noises.

I waved the map at them.

"What happened to chasing down the secret of the golden turkey eggs or whatever?!" Then, in a much quieter voice, I whispered, "I was finally getting into all this ridiculousness . . ."

"That map has been in some dusty old crate for a hundred years, Hunter," Lloyd said, happily trotting toward the nearest hot-dog cart. "Its secrets can wait until we've had lunch."

Begrudgingly, I tucked the map back into Harry's back-pack, and Harry threw our newly discovered turkey-foot key in there, too. Then I joined Harry and Lloyd in line at the hot-dog cart. I don't even eat meat, but I had to admit—fries sounded good after all the chaos of the day.

There were about ten people ahead of us in line, and I spent most of the wait looking around nervously to see if Reginald California had found us. Lloyd and Harry, on the other hand, spent most of the wait picking the remaining flying-suit feathers out of each other's hair.

Finally, we reached the front of the line, and Reginald was nowhere in sight. Until . . .

"I've got you brats now!" the hot-dog vendor said, reaching over the cart to grab the front of Lloyd's shirt with one hand while balancing a pair of chili dogs in the other. Reginald wasn't looking for us—he'd already found us!

"If you don't let Lloyd go, I'll scream," I angrily whispered to him. "Maybe you could play it off dressed as a security guard, but I don't think people would take kindly to a hot-dog vendor attacking three helpless kids."

"'Helpless'!" Reginald scoffed back at me. "You three tiny terrors have nearly ruined decades of well-laid plans from the Order of the Snood."

Lloyd wiggled in Reginald's grasp, but Reginald hung on tight. Behind us, the line was already growing impatient.

"Maybe your Order isn't so *orderly* if three sixth

graders can mess up your plans, Snood dude," Lloyd replied, making matters worse.

Reginald pulled him closer, and the people behind us in line were definitely starting to notice something was up.

"I will be the one to uncover the untold riches and secret history of Benjamin Franklin, you frustrating fledgling!" Reginald growled.

I looked to Harry to see if he had a plan, but Harry was torn between concern for Lloyd and hunger for the hot dogs in Reginald's other hand. It looked like it was up to me to save the day.

"He may be frustrating, but he's my frustrating friend!" I yelled as I reached for the mustard bottle. Reginald California turned to look at me, and I squirted a heaping helping of the condiment right in his face. He dropped Lloyd—and the hot dogs—at once.

"Gah, my eyes!" he screamed. "I have a very mild mustard allergy, you awful child!"

"Maybe you shouldn't have disguised yourself as a hotdog vendor, then!" I shouted back, grabbing both boys and pulling them along with me.

While the crowd behind us looked on in confusion—and while Reginald California tried to wipe mustard out of his eyes and mustache—we made our getaway, sprinting toward the Washington Monument and the Lincoln Memorial.

"Fast thinking, Tini," Lloyd said. "Only, couldn't you have saved the hot dogs, too?"

For a second, I thought about tripping Lloyd and letting him fend for himself with California. Of all the ungrateful—

"Don't worry, Lloyd!" Harry said, cutting off my thought. "I got them!" Harry produced two hot dogs, each with a mild coating of dirt, which he quickly blew off.

The dirt didn't slow them down, though, and they each shoveled one into their mouths as we passed the Smithsonian Castle, sprinted along Jefferson Drive, looked both ways before crossing 14th Street Street, and finally slowed to a stop in front of the Washington Monument, a huge obelisk that rises into the sky.

By then, we were all out of breath, and Lloyd and Harry had stomachaches from eating while they ran.

"So nauseous," Lloyd said between heavy breaths of air. "But so delicious . . . and so worth it . . ."

I shielded my eyes with the back of my hand and looked down the rest of the Mall toward the Lincoln Memorial. Just getting this far had worn us out, and we still had *twice* as far to go before reaching the giant stone Lincoln in his giant stone chair.

"Guys," I said, doing my best to catch my own breath. "Lincoln is . . . too far. We can't . . . outrun Reginald . . . that long."

"Maybe we can . . . out-pedal him?" Harry offered, holding his cramped stomach and pointing behind me.

A bicycle rental stand. There were three of us, and two bikes left to rent. Someone was going to ride in the basket, and it *wasn't* going to be me.

CHAPTER 13

"What do you *mean* you don't have any cash?" I asked, staring down at Lloyd's and Harry's empty out-turned pockets. "How were you going to pay for the hot dogs?"

"We figured you'd float us," Lloyd said with a shrug. "You know we're good for it. C'mon. *C'mon.*"

"Yeah, we *always* pay our debts," Harry added. "We've given out *hundreds* of IOUs, right, Lloyd? Dozens, even!"

"And have you paid back any of those IOUs?" I asked.

Lloyd tapped his forehead.

"We will, Hunter, once we cash in those shiny golden eggs," he said. "Trust me—until then, they're all catalogued up here in this unbreakable vault I like to call . . . my noggin."

I didn't have time to point out the flaws in Harry and Lloyd's debt system. We needed to get across the rest of the National Mall to the next marker on the map before Reginald California caught up with us.

I asked the bike-rental person if they had any other bikes left, but all she had were the two in front of us and a child-sized tricycle in the back that Lloyd tried to make a serious case for. With a deep sigh, I forked over the cash to rent the two adult bikes, promising (aka lying) that we wouldn't ride two to a bike. Once we were out of the rental person's earshot, Harry and Lloyd commenced a game of rock paper scissors to decide who got to pedal and who had to sit in the basket.

"Rock tears right through paper," Lloyd said, either because he was bluffing or because he didn't actually know the rules of the game.

"Aww, no fair—I already had to ride on your back when we went flying," Harry responded. "I wanted to do all the pedaling this time."

"All the pedaling, you say?" Lloyd cracked a grin. "Well, if you insist, good buddy. I wouldn't want to take that privilege away from you."

Harry's smile lit up. He didn't realize Lloyd had just tricked him into doing the hard work, but he looked so happy, I didn't have the heart to break it to him.

"Now that that's settled," I said, getting situated on my own bike, "let's get going."

No sooner did we kick off on our bikes—mine sailing smoothly, Harry and Lloyd's wobbling as they tried to find their balance together—did I get another call from . . .

"Zoey, hey, can't talk right now, really busy!" I spoke into the phone, pushing the pedals as fast as I could while still avoiding all the tourists around us.

"Tini, don't you dare hang up on me!" she responded. I could hear Mrs. McCormick telling her what to say in the background, though of course, Zoey was putting her own spin on it. "We've been looking all over the museum for you, Hairbrained, and Loser."

"*Harry and Lloyd*," I corrected her. Before this trip, I would have been making up names for them, too, but spending the last few crazy hours with them was making me feel a little more protective of the doofuses.

"Whatever. Just tell me where you are before Mrs. McCormick mobilizes a search party and they lock down all of Washington, D.C."

I bit my lip, thinking hard about whether I should explain what was going on or try to buy us some more time. That's when I looked over and saw Harry and Lloyd pedaling straight for the base of the Washington Monument.

"Turn, Harry, turn!" I shouted. "You're going to run right into the Washington Monu—"

Before I could finish my sentence, the front wheel of the boys' bike hit a ledge, and both tumbled right over the handlebars, landing inches from the monument.

"Wait, Tini, did you say—" Zoey managed to get out

before I hung up on her. Apologies to my bestie—I was in it too deep to quit now, and those boys needed me.

A crowd started to gather, but Lloyd stood up—or wobbled up, more like it—and shooed them away.

"Nothing to see here, folks! Just two healthy young Americans, admiring our history . . . up close and personal."

I was helping Harry up from the ground when I heard an engine rev and someone shout, "Halt!" behind us. I turned around, expecting to see some sort of security guard, but instead it was much, *much* worse.

Reginald California, clearly recovered from the mustard incident, was headed straight for us on a motorcycle! Apparently this Order of the Snood had some real resources at their disposal, and Reginald was sick of being outwitted by three preteens. The only thing we still had in our favor was that the Mall was crowded, so Reginald couldn't get his bike up to full speed. Still, it wouldn't take him long to catch up to us at this rate.

I dusted Harry off and shoved him in the basket of the bike, since he was in no shape to pedal.

"Wait a second. I'm the basket boy," Lloyd protested. I didn't even answer with words—I just gave him my meanest, most serious glare. He gulped and stood at attention, saluting me like I was his drill sergeant. "Sir, yes, sir!" he said, and took his position on the bike.

With Harry rubbing his head (I couldn't imagine that the number of times these guys had hit their heads

throughout this whole saga was going to *help* their person-
alities), Lloyd and I raced as quickly as we could along the
Reflecting Pool, with Reginald California speeding along behind
us on his motorcycle.

Just when it looked like —

CHAPTER 13

AND A HALF

Yeah, sorry to cut you off there, Tini-beany, but you are just not capturing the action, the excitement, the thrill of the chase. Let your old pal Lloyd tell this part of the story, yeah?

So there I was, pedaling for dear life, the wind rushing against my handsome, intelligent, charming face as our feather-brained foe gained on us—

CHAPTER 14

I can't believe Lloyd ripped pages right out of *my* story to staple in his version of events, which is certainly . . . exaggerated, let's say that. What he did get right is that Reginald California would have caught us in no time if it wasn't for all the people around slowing him down.

By the time we got to the far end of the Reflecting Pool, in front of the steps leading up to the Lincoln Memorial, Reginald was hot on our heels (or wheels, as the case may have been).

We dropped our bikes and started to run up the steps, but then Lloyd stopped cold.

"It's no good, pals," he said, solemnly. "We need . . . *a distraction.*"

"Aww man," Harry replied, his shoulders slumping. "Just tell me what I have to do, Lloyd. But no more space shuttles!"

Then the unthinkable happened.

"Not this time, Harry," Lloyd said. "I'll be the decoy now."

Lloyd lifted his chin up proudly, and a single tear ran down Harry's cheek. The two embraced like brothers, and I saw behind them that Reginald California was using this touching moment to gain ground.

"This is really sweet, guys," I said, butting in. "But it's not going to mean anything if we don't get to the next spot on the map before the motorcycle mustache man catches up with us!"

Lloyd spun Harry around and dug into his backpack. He pulled out his own dinged-up, disheveled workbook and rolled it tight, until it looked just like the map.

"Don't worry, Tini," he scream-whispered to me, "I didn't grab the *real* map!"

"I got that, Lloyd," I replied, shushing him. "Now go do whatever you're planning to do!"

As Harry and I ran up the stairs toward the giant Lincoln statue, Lloyd stepped back down to the edge of the Reflecting Pool. Against my own advice to hurry, I couldn't help but turn back to watch Lloyd and Reginald California meet face-to-face again.

"Out of my way, fool!" Reginald yelled at Lloyd, stepping off his motorcycle like the intimidating bad guy in a spy movie.

"Not so fast, birdbrain," Lloyd responded, holding up the tightly rolled fake map in his hands. "Unless you want your turkey map to go for a little swim."

Reginald just scoffed at him.

"That clearly isn't the actual map to Ben Franklin's vault. Why would you and your little friends destroy your only chance to uncover its long-lost secrets?"

Lloyd pinched the end of his nose and stepped closer to the edge of the Reflecting Pool. The rest of his threat to Reginald California came out sounding super nasally as a result, but it was still effective.

"I think you should know by now," Lloyd said calmly, "that it's impossible to guess why we do *any* of the things we do."

And with that, Lloyd Christmas jumped right into the Reflecting Pool, one of the most famous bodies of water in America, face-first.

"The map!" Reginald shouted, reaching out to grab it before it could get soaked. He missed by inches and lost his balance. With a big SPLASH! Reginald joined Lloyd in the water, as onlookers gathered from all sides and waved over security guards to help them.

And it did look like they needed help – both Lloyd and Reginald California thrashed around in the water like their lives depended on it.

"Wow, some Turkey Orderer you are," Lloyd said between gulps of air. "You're an old man, and you can't even swim!"

Reginald splashed back at Lloyd, trying and failing to swim closer toward him.

"I'm not old—I'm in my early midforties!" Reginald went under for a second, then reappeared, spitting water out from behind his mustache. "And I grew up in a temperate desert climate—swimming was never a practical concern! What's your excuse?"

Lloyd bobbed under now, too, and came back up trying to do some bizarre version of a backstroke.

"I fell into a Port-O-Toilet as a toddler and vowed never to swim again!"

This horrifying memory was thankfully cut short when a group of park rangers finally made it over to the scene and grabbed Reginald out of the water. As this happened, Lloyd stopped thrashing long enough to realize . . . that the Reflecting Pool is about two feet deep at its deepest point.

"Oh, hey, I can stand up here."

"Why, you little—"

Reginald tried to break free, but the guards held him back. Lloyd used the confusion (which was basically a distraction on top of a distraction for another distraction at this point) to disappear into the crowd of onlookers and snake his way over to the stairs of the Lincoln Memorial.

While all the tourists and visitors watched a soaking, kicking, screaming man with a substantial mustache get carried away, Lloyd skipped over to us, proud as could be.

There was only one problem: Harry and I had the map open to see where the turkey-foot key unlocked the

next secret, and Lloyd was still soaking wet. As he leaned over to see the map for himself, the water from his hair dripped all over it, and the decades-old paper fell apart in our hands.

"Oops."

CHAPTER 15

"Nothing," I said, sitting down on the cold stone floor of the monument. "I'm going to get in *so much* trouble, and it was all for nothing."

Harry, still holding the soggy mess that just minutes ago was a secret map, crouched down next to me. He looked toward me, but I just stared off into the distance of the Reflecting Pool, reflecting on all the bad choices that had led me here.

"Aww, don't say that, Tini," Harry said, putting a wet, pulpy hand on my shoulder. "Life is all about the journey, not about going anywhere."

I couldn't help but laugh.

"'Life is about the journey, not the destination'—that's the saying," I corrected him. I wasn't nice about it, either. "Do you ever get *anything* right, Harry?"

I could see the hurt in his eyes, but my lips didn't stop moving.

"Ever since we got paired together for this trip, you two have brought nonstop chaos and annoyance into my life, dragging me from one outrageous situation to the next!"

Now I was heated, and I got back up on my feet, pacing around the Lincoln Memorial. Harry was still giving me puppy-dog eyes, and I couldn't read Lloyd's expression at all.

"All I wanted to do was visit some sites and get back on the bus home, where I could go back to forgetting you two exist! Instead, I've been chased all over the National Mall by a strange man obsessed with turkeys, I've been part of a plot to steal from *multiple* museums, and I've spent the day running all over the capital following bird clues on a map you just *ruined* at the finish line!"

I paused for breath and noticed that Harry had tears in his eyes. Lloyd patted his friend's back, and even though I was angrier than anything at these two, I pretty much instantly regretted most of what I had just said.

"We just felt sorry for you," Harry said, trying not to cry.

I was taken aback.

"Sorry for *me*? Why would *you two* feel sorry for *me*?"

Harry looked down at his feet.

"Well, the girl you always hang out with chose that other kid as her trip buddy, and you didn't seem to have anyone left to pair up with, so . . ."

Lloyd stepped in to finish Harry's sentence.

"So Harry told Mrs. McCormick that you could join our group."

I'll admit it—I was speechless. This whole time that Harry and Lloyd had been getting on my nerves and running me around the National Mall in this big crazy plot, they thought they were *doing me a favor.* And they didn't do it because I've ever been nice to them—they did it because they thought it was the right thing to do.

"I . . . don't know what to say," I stammered. "Harry, I'm so sor—"

Lloyd huffed and turned Harry away from me by the shoulder.

"We don't accept your apology."

Harry turned right back around and came in for a hug.

"Sure we do, Lloyd," he said, smushing me in his arms. I'm pretty sure Harry had needed a shower even *before* we ran all over town, but I held my breath and ignored that for the moment. "We forgive you, Tini. We all say things we don't mean when we're mad."

Harry was right, but he also reminded me *why* I was upset.

"Thanks, guys, and thanks for inviting me into your group. But the map is still ruined, which means we can't find the rest of the clues leading to Ben Franklin's secret treasure or whatever."

"The secret treasure of countless golden turkey eggs . . . right," Lloyd chimed in, still certain about his interpretation of the map.

Harry pulled the turkey-foot-shaped key out of his backpack.

"We still have this!" he exclaimed.

"Yeah, but look how big this monument is," I replied. "It could fit anywhere."

Harry stared at the key and scratched his head.

"Well . . . it's got a turkey foot on it . . . so maybe it goes in this big guy's foot, too?"

The "big guy" Harry was talking about was the giant statue of Abraham Lincoln that looks out over the Reflecting Pool.

"You're thinking too obviously, my simple friend," Lloyd chimed in, making his way over toward the statue's oversized feet. "Millions of people visit this statue every year. Surely, someone would notice by now if there was just a keyhole out in plain . . . sight . . ."

Lloyd started to trail off, and I noticed he was staring at the part of Lincoln's right foot that extends past the base of the statue. Without finishing his sentence, Lloyd crouched down to look at the underside of the statue's shoe.

"Scratch that," Lloyd said. "Harry's right."

"What do you mean, 'Harry's right'?" I asked, incredulous.

"I don't know what to tell you, Tini—Harry guessed it. Somehow no one's ever bothered to look, because there is a keyhole right in the bottom of this guy's big old shoe."

Lloyd had to be pulling my leg. I took the key from

Harry and stomped over to the statue. The tourists who got tied up in Reginald California's splashing and thrashing hadn't made their way back up the memorial yet, so we had the area around the statue to ourselves for a moment.

I bent down, expecting to see flat stone. But instead . . . I saw a keyhole, plain as day.

"Well, what do you know."

I looked at Harry, who gave me an encouraging thumbs-up. Then I slid the key into the lock and turned it. There was a sound like rock grinding against rock, and then the floor dropped out from below our feet, plummeting us all into darkness.

CHAPTER 16

"I'm too young to go out like this!" Lloyd shouted. "I've got so much more mayhem to cau—"

Before he could finish yelling, the three of us landed on a stone floor, maybe five or six feet down. A surprising fall, but not nearly as bad as it could have been.

"Oh, that wasn't so terrible."

I looked up and saw something that made the situation much worse, though: The panel of the floor that slid open was now sliding shut, potentially trapping us beneath the Lincoln Memorial forever.

"Quick, don't let it close!" I yelled, but it was already too late. Within moments, we were plunged into total darkness. I reached for my cell phone to light up the area, but before I could turn it on, torches lit up on the walls around us.

Harry, Lloyd, and I looked around and tried to get our bearings. We were in a small stone room, and the torches continued down a winding staircase carved out of rock.

With the trapdoor above shut and too high for us to reach, I led the boys in the only direction we could go . . . down.

"Hopefully, we don't need the key to get anywhere else," I said. "I think it's still hanging in Lincoln's foot."

"Oh, that's who that guy was?" Harry asked. "I *knew* he looked familiar."

As we continued down the staircase, Lloyd sniffed the air.

"Smells like feathers, my friends," he said. "We're close."

I thought it smelled like a musty old tomb underground, where we'd never get cell reception or be heard from ever again, but reactions may vary, I guess.

About a hundred steps down, we finally hit the bottom of the passageway. We must have been a few stories underground now, probably at the same level as the subbasement under the Smithsonian where we first started our turkey quest.

The stairs opened up into another small stone room, but this one had a large ornate door at the other end. Lloyd rushed over to try the handle, but it was locked tight. He wiggled and yanked on it and gave it a kick or three for good measure, but it didn't budge.

"Wait a second," I said, pointing to the top of the door-frame. "'The Order of the Snood'—that's the secret society Reginald California kept going on about!"

On closer inspection, the door was covered in all sorts of turkey-related carvings and symbols. And above the big lock in the middle was the symbol of a turkey's beak.

"But . . . we didn't find anything related to a turkey's beak," I said. "It must have been part of the map we didn't get to. Maybe we followed the quest out of order?"

Harry grabbed the soggy remnants of the map out of his bag, but there was no chance of getting anything useful out of it now.

"So . . . I guess it really is over, then," he said sadly. "Maybe if we pound on the ceiling real hard in the other room, someone will let us out."

Lloyd pushed us both out of the way and stepped toward the door.

"We've come too far to give up now, my good buddies," he said. "Besides, what did I say earlier? We must become one with the majestic turkey if we expect them to lay their shining golden eggs for us. So if this door requires a beak . . ."

Lloyd bent over until his face was eye level with the lock on the door. He slowly leaned forward and inserted his nose into the open spot on the lock.

"Lloyd, don't—this is a horrible idea!" I said, trying to stop him before he broke his beak—er, nose.

"That's never held me back before!" he said, grunting as he twisted his head to the left. Amazingly, I heard the lock start to turn.

"Almost there, Lloyd!" Harry said, clapping and cheering his friend on. Lloyd kept grunting under the strain. I was sure his nose was going to give before the lock did, but then I heard a "CLICK" and Lloyd fell forward as the door *whooshed* open before him.

Harry and I both rushed to his side, but Lloyd was already massaging his nose back into place when we got there.

"Guess the old schnoz is good for something after all, eh?" he asked, but Harry and I weren't paying attention to him anymore. Instead, we were looking up at a giant portrait hanging on the wall in front of us.

At first glance, it looked like any old American portrait of a man in a powdered wig and fancy clothes. But the big, bold inscription at the bottom of the frame confirmed our assumption about who we were looking at:

BENJAMIN FRANKLIN, FOUNDER OF THE ORDER OF THE SNOOD.

I looked at Harry and then at Lloyd. This was it—the secret history Reginald California had been looking for. All of California's rantings were *real*, which means this room could be the discovery of the decade—no, the century. Maybe of several centuries!

"Do you know what this means?" I asked the boys.

Lloyd stood up and posed in front of the picture, laughing and pointing a thumb back at it.

"Yeah, this old guy looks just like my grandma!"

I looked at the rest of the room around us, and it was obvious that everything present was connected to some corner of history. As the boys started to ruffle through the priceless artifacts, I spotted drafts of the Declaration of Independence with signatures I've never heard of before, turkey-emblazoned documents signed by Benjamin Franklin, and even a dartboard with George Washington's portrait painted onto it.

Everything down there could change the world as we knew it, and Lloyd and Harry were goofing around like they had just stumbled into their neighbor's attic. Lloyd was using a pair of wooden dentures like a puppet, while Harry tried on a military jacket that must have dated back to the Revolutionary War.

I let out a laugh, realizing that these two had *no idea* what we had stumbled into.

"That's the spirit!" Lloyd said, laughing along with me. "If we don't get a secret farm full of golden turkeys, at least we can have some fun with this old junk."

I kept giggling as I wandered around the room, spotting artifacts that would break our history books in half, when I heard what I thought was an echo at first. Only, when I stopped laughing, the echo *didn't* stop. Which could only mean one thing: We weren't alone down there.

Lloyd is my hero

If you have discovered this hidden room, then I must offer my hearty and patriotic congratulations on solving my puzzle. I can only hope you were gentle with Petunia when removing the codex from her eternally preserved gullet. What you will find in my secret chambers is not an alternative history of these fine United States, but a more complete documentation of their founding. My influence on our burgeoning country runs deep, though I fear the history books might reduce me to some silly side note in my story, such as that awful shock I received from my kite during that terrible thunderstorm—a ghastly time, and one I hope will not follow me beyond the grave. Please treat the artifacts here with the greatest of care and respect, as I have gathered this treasure trove for the purpose of educating future generations clever enough to uncover the deepest truths of our nation.

Yours in the utmost confidence,

Benjamin Franklin

CHAPTER 17

"Quiet—do you hear that?" I said, hushing the boys.

Lloyd grabbed the wooden dentures from Harry and mimicked speaking to me with them.

"Hear what, good chap!" he said, the wood clacking in his hand.

"I mean it—I think someone else is down here!"

That got even Lloyd to be quiet. Then we definitely heard it: footsteps coming down the stairs. It didn't take long to figure out who it was, either.

"You perfidious preteens!" Reginald California shouted, the sound of his voice echoing down to us. "You'll not foil the Order of the Snood today!"

Harry, Lloyd, and I looked at one another and then at the room around us. Every corner was full of documents, paintings, statues, and other artifacts, but there was no exit besides the staircase Reginald was coming down.

"We can't let Reginald get his hands on all these secrets," I said. "There's no telling what he wants with them, but it *definitely* isn't good."

"You're absolutely right," Lloyd responded, still talking through his denture puppet.

"But I don't see another way out, and we can't carry all this ourselves, anyway," I said. "The history down here is priceless — we can't just lock it away forever again . . . can we?"

Harry put his hand on my shoulder.

"A wise friend once told me: A journey of a thousand miles starts with the friends you make along the way.'"

I thought about correcting him, but he wasn't exactly wrong (even if his quotes were).

"I think I know what you mean, Harry," I replied. "We didn't do all of this because we knew we'd find some hidden treasure or secret—"

"No, I really thought we were going to find turkeys that laid golden eggs," Lloyd interjected.

"And I was mostly running away from that California guy," Harry added.

"We *did* it," I continued, "because we all got swept up in the adventure of it. Me included, even though I kept telling myself I was being dragged along or was just trying to keep you two from creating an international incident."

"Wouldn't be my first!" Lloyd added.

Reginald California's footsteps were getting closer, so I took one last look at the secrets of Ben Franklin's vault and then nudged the boys toward the big wooden door.

"C'mon, we've got to get this shut again before he gets down here."

Harry and I pulled both sides of the heavy wooden door shut while Lloyd flexed his nose back and forth. Reginald ended up making it down the last steps just in time to catch a glimpse of what lay beyond the door as "SLAM," we pulled it closed. Before Reginald could grab him, Lloyd inserted his nose into the beak lock and twisted it in the opposite direction, locking it shut once more.

"No!" Reginald screamed, flying forward toward the door. We all three moved out of the way, and he face-planted in the dust. As Reginald scrambled to his feet, I got a good look at what he was wearing: Imagine if someone took the gaudiest Thanksgiving decorations you've ever seen and stuck them on a high school marching band's uniform.

"The Order of the Snood has searched for Benjamin Franklin's hidden vault for decades!" he cried. "I donned our secret uniform so this moment would be *perfect*, but you brats have ruined everything – everything!"

Reginald tried to force his own nose into the beak lock, but it was too big to fit, and his mustache kept getting in the way. He turned toward us with his hands outstretched and a desperate look on his face.

"The map – give me the map. I must find the location of the beak key. It's not too late!"

Harry reached into his backpack, pulled out the soaking wad of paper that used to be the map, and then plopped it into Reginald's waiting hands. It took Reginald a moment to realize what he was holding, and then he let out the loudest, deepest scream I'd ever heard.

I used the moment to push Harry and Lloyd toward the stairs, and we ran up them as fast as we could as Reginald's cries echoed along the stone walls.

When we reached the top, I saw that the stone panel was open again! Harry and Lloyd boosted me up so I could grab on to the edge and pull myself up. Then I reached back down to help Harry climb up. It took a few jumps, but we grabbed hold of Lloyd, too, and all three of us flopped back on the cool stone of the Lincoln Memorial.

There was no time to relax, though – we could hear Reginald California running up the stairs below us.

Lloyd moved to turn the key and close the floor panel, but I slapped his hand away.

"Lloyd! We can't trap him down there."

"Oh, sure, sure, wouldn't dream of it . . ."

Instead, we all hid around the corner of the statue, peeking out at the opening. Reginald California made a running jump and grabbed on to the ledge, pulling himself over and growling as he looked around for us.

Harry and Lloyd poked out from behind the statue and stuck their tongues out at Reginald, drawing his attention while I snuck around the other way and turned the key in Lincoln's right foot, shutting the panel once more. When Reginald turned around to try to stop me, I gave the key a sharp kick, breaking it off in the lock. Now *no one* could access the secrets hidden below the memorial.

"You will pay for that!" Reginald California screamed, looming over us. "So swears the Order of the Snood!"

CHAPTER 18

For half a second, I was actually afraid of this turkey-obsessed loon. Then I heard someone shout, "Freeze, chicken boy!" from the steps below, and I looked over to see a whole squad of park rangers walking toward Reginald with nets outstretched.

"Are you kids okay?" one of them asked, looking in our direction. "We got reports of a giant rabid bird flying around the Mall earlier and came here to investigate."

"I'm no bird, you nincompoops!" Reginald shouted, turning to face the nets. "I am a high-ranking member of the Order of the Snood, and I will not stand for—"

"SWOOSH!" One of the park rangers nearest to Reginald swung her net over Reginald's head, cutting his threats short. While he struggled to untangle himself, two more park rangers managed to grab him from behind and tie his hands up. It seemed that this big angry bird had been grounded.

"You brats haven't seen the last of me!" Reginal shouted

as the rangers led him away. "The Order of the Snood will fly again!"

"You Snood, you lose!" Harry replied, laughing at his own joke.

One of the few park rangers who weren't involved with carting Reginald California away came over to make sure we were all okay, but she barely got a word out before she was interrupted.

"These are my students . . . unfortunately," Mrs. McCormick sighed, climbing the last step up to the monument. I looked behind her and saw our entire class waiting down by the Reflecting Pool. "I'll handle them from here, if that's okay with you."

The park ranger nodded and walked away, leaving us to face Mrs. McCormick's wrath.

"Hunter. Dunne. *Christmas*," Mrs. McCormick said, looking us up and down one at a time.

"How did you find us?" I asked.

"Miss Han heard you say something about the Washington Monument," she replied, pointing down at Zoey, who was standing with the rest of the class. "From there, we followed the confusion and chaos. That's usually a good way to find Harry and Lloyd." The boys smiled at this "compliment."

"Let's make this as easy on each other as possible," Mrs. McCormick said. "Did any of you break anything?"

I pocketed the half of the key that was not permanently stuck in Abraham Lincoln's foot.

"Not any bones," I said.

"Did any of you *take* anything?"

I looked at Lloyd, who still had a feather in his hair from the flying suit.

"Nothing . . . that will be missed," he replied.

Mrs. McCormick sighed.

"Did any of you run into trouble with law enforcement?"

Harry smiled.

"Ooh, I know this one — not any *real* law enforcement."

Mrs. McCormick stared us down again. She was silent for a long time, and I started to get nervous. But then her shoulders slouched, and she turned back toward the steps.

"Good enough for me," she said. "I don't get paid enough to ask more than that. C'mon, let's get back to the class — and stay together this time, *please.*"

I was stunned for a second. Were we really going to get away with all the trouble we'd gotten into?

"Oh, and, Hunter?" she said, turning back to me. I swallowed hard. *Here it comes*, I thought. *I'm totally getting detention or suspended or expelled or —*

"Good job keeping those two in line. They can be a handful."

I exhaled.

"And, Harry and Lloyd," she continued, "I'm glad your offer to buddy up with Tini went . . . well enough."

"Oh, sure, no problem at all," Lloyd responded. "It was

just like hanging out with my grandma all day, only Tini complains more."

I was about to roll my eyes, but Lloyd winked at me, and I couldn't help but laugh.

Mrs. McCormick led us down the steps and back to the rest of the class. Everyone was abuzz trying to figure out what had happened, and Lloyd wasn't shy with the details, but I could tell right away that no one believed him. I guess that was one of the perks of living such a ridiculous life — it was almost too good to be true.

I was listening to Lloyd and Harry explain (and exaggerate) the story when Zoey tapped me on the shoulder.

"Tini."

"Zoey."

"Don't tell me you're still mad at me," she said.

"Mad at you? You're mad at *me*," I responded.

"Oh, please, the longest I've been mad at you is four days, two hours, and thirty-five minutes, and our silly fight the other day wasn't *that* big a deal."

"Four days, two hours, and thirty-three minutes," I corrected her. She rolled her eyes and gave me a hug.

"Okay, now spill — what have you and the bogus brothers been up to all day?"

I looked back at Harry and Lloyd, who were spinning around, re-creating a much more fanciful version of their flight through the air. I had seen it all firsthand, and even I had trouble believing it happened.

"You know, Zoey," I said. "They're actually pretty cool when you get to know them. They're weird—don't get me wrong—but *cool*, too."

"If you say so, Tini. But seriously, what happened today? Why were you running all over the National Mall, and who was that weird guy in the bird suit?"

I took a deep breath and thought about how I was going to explain any of this.

"Zoey, you're not going to believe me, but it all started with a stuffed turkey—"

Before I could go into more detail, Mrs. McCormick and the other chaperones gathered the whole class together for a group photo in front of the Lincoln Memorial. Zoey pulled me close, but I waved over Harry and Lloyd, too.

I needed a photo with *all* my friends in it to remember *this* unbelievable weekend.

The Lincoln Memorial!!!

Mrs. McCormick and
the class in front of
The Smithsonian!!!

Zoe and I made up!!!

NO WAY—YOU're
going to camp.
too, Tini? See
YOU there!
—Harry

Steve Foxe is the author of more than fifty children's and comics books for properties including Marvel's Spider-Ham, Pokémon, Batman, Transformers, Adventure Time, Steven Universe, and Grumpy Cat. He lives in Queens with his partner and their dog, who is named after a cartoon character. Find out more at stevefoxe.com.

Shadia Amin is a Colombian comic artist currently living in the U.S. Her art aims to capture the fun of superheroes, fantasy, and life itself. Her works include BOOM!'s *The Amazing World of Gumball: The Storm*, and Oni-Lion Forge's *Aggretsuko*, as well as collaborations on anthologies like *Alloy* from Ascend Comics and *Votes for Women* from Little Red Bird Press.